A Cat Called Max

Max's Amazing Summer

Barron's Arch Book Series

A Cat Called Max

Max's Amazing Summer

Terrance Dicks

Illustrated by Toni Goffe

First edition for the United States, Canada, and the Philippines published 1992 by Barron's Educational Series, Inc.

First published 1991 by Piccadilly Press Ltd., London, England

All inquiries should be addressed to:
Barron's Educational Series, Inc.
250 Wireless Boulevard
Hauppauge, New York 11788

International Standard Book No. 0-8120-4819-9

Library of Congress Catalog Card No. 91-30745

Library of Congress Cataloging-in-Publication Data

Dicks, Terrance.
    Max's amazing summer / Terrance Dicks ; illustrated by Toni Goffe.
—1st ed. for the U.S., Canada, and the Phillipines.
        p. cm.—(Barron's arch book series) (A Cat called Max)
    "First published 1991 by Piccadilly Press Ltd., London, England"—
T.p. verso.
    Summary: Max, the sophisticated talking cat, must save the town from unusually hot weather and strange giant insects when a greedy member of the garden club starts manufacturing a new kind of fertilizer.
    ISBN 0-8120-4819-9
    [1. Cats—Fiction. 2. Science fiction.] I. Goffe, Toni, ill. II Title.
III. Series: Barron's arch book series. IV Series: Dicks, Terrance. Cat called Max.
PZ7.D5627Mb   1992   91-30745
[Fic]—dc20   CIP
                                                                          AC

PRINTED IN THE UNITED STATES OF AMERICA
2345   9770   987654321

CONTENTS

Chapter One

Heat Wave

"I don't like it," said Max. "All this sunshine just isn't natural. Something very strange is going on!"

Timmy was quite happy with the weather. He was lying on an air mattress in his bathing suit covered with suntan oil, toasting gently in the sun.

His little sister Samantha—Sam for short—was in her bathing suit too. She

1

was over by the ivy-covered fence, happily splashing away in one of those inflatable wading pools. "Timmy play!" she yelled.

Samantha's idea of a game was for Timmy to sit there while she threw water over him with her little plastic pail. If he threw any back, she screamed blue murder.

Timmy's dad was watering the garden, which for once was a blaze of color. "I've never seen the garden look so good," he said happily. "And you should see the size of my pumpkins. I'm trying a new fertilizer. Wonderful stuff."

Everyone was enjoying the fine weather.

Everyone but Max.

He was sitting in a patch of cool shade just outside the kitchen door, looking thoroughly fed up.

Max was a cat. He was a big, handsome

animal, all black except for a patch of white just under his chin.

But Max was no ordinary cat. He talked, he walked on his hind legs, and he had a number of amazing and unusual powers.

Just now he was feeling grumpy. "This

is supposed to be summer. Where are the thunderstorms? It's not supposed to be hot and sunny all the time!"

Timmy's mother came out into the garden with a tray full of glasses of lemonade. She passed one to Max who took it with his usual politeness. "Thank you, dear lady. Most refreshing!"

"Cheer up, Max," said Timmy, sitting up to gulp his lemonade. "I'm enjoying the hot weather."

"That is quite obvious," said Max. "Personally, I fail to see the pleasure in lying there sizzling like a human sausage!"

"What's wrong with a little sunshine?"

"A little sunshine!" said Max, waving a copy of the local newspaper. "Do you realize that this has been the hottest place on record for weeks and weeks?"

Suddenly Samantha screamed in terror. "No, go away! Go away!"

Everyone turned to look, but it was Max who acted.

His eyes glowed a bright fierce green and Samantha shot right up out of the little pool like a leaping dolphin, landing in her astonished mother's arms.

In one giant jump Max was beside the plastic pool, ready to confront the unknown menace.

Timmy was on his feet too by now, and his father had grabbed a rake.

They both caught a glimpse of something round and furry, scurrying away into the ivy.

Timmy's mom was trying to calm the dripping, sobbing Samantha. "It's all right, dear. It's gone now. What was it? What frightened you?"

"Could have been a stray cat," said Mr. Tompkins. "No offense, Max!"

"Sam's not scared of cats," said Timmy. "Or dogs either, come to think of it. She always rushes up and tries to hug them."

"Perhaps it was a rat," suggested Mrs. Tompkins, wrapping Samantha in a towel.

"*Not* a cat! *Not* a rat!" roared Samantha. "Bath creepy-crawly!"

"She means a spider," said Timmy in amazement. "They get into the bathtub sometimes. Sam hates them."

"Spider!" roared Samantha. "Great big spider!"

"All right, it was a spider," said her mother soothingly. "We'll have to call you Little Miss Muffet, won't we?"

She recited the old nursery rhyme as she carried Samantha into the house. "Little Miss Muffet sat on a tuffet..."

"Could have been a hedgehog," said Timmy's dad, as he went off down the garden path.

"I wonder what frightened her," said Timmy uneasily.

"She told you, my dear fellow!"

"But it can't have been a spider. I only caught a glimpse—it was much too big."

"How does the rest of that nursery rhyme go?" asked Max.

"Along came a spider and sat down beside her,

And frightened Miss Muffet away."

Suddenly the words of the old rhyme sounded strangely sinister.

"I saw the thing quite clearly," said Max. "Your sister was frightened by a spider the size of a football. Now will you believe that something strange is going on?"

Chapter Two

Terror in the Shed

Max picked up the local newspaper
again. "Just listen to this." He began
reading it out loud. "'Local man in
hospital after mystery wasp sting.' And
again here. 'Boy bitten by mystery dog in
cellar.' And this one. 'Mystery animals
destroy grocery's food supplies.'"

"Well, that's just the newspapers, isn't
it?" asked Timmy uneasily. "They
always have to make everything
sound sensational."

Max shook his head. "These stories really are mysterious. The man who was stung insists it was one huge wasp—but there was as much poison in his body as if he'd been stung by a whole swarm. The boy heard a noise in the cellar, went down to look and something bit him. He says it was a rat—but the bite marks are so big the doctor said it must have been a dog. Whatever it was, it got away. And whatever broke into the grocer's store-

room ripped open lots of packages and
ate huge amounts of sugar."

"Ants love sugar," said Timmy,
and shivered.

Suddenly they heard a yell from
the garden.

"That's Dad," gasped Timmy.

Max ran down the garden path, Timmy
close behind him.

They found Mr. Tompkins staring
down at his pumpkin bed.

"Look at that!" he yelled. "Just look at that!"

Timmy looked hard at the pumpkins and saw that they all had big bites taken out of them.

His father shook his head. "I've never seen anything like it. I mean you always have trouble with garden pests, slugs and that kind of thing, but bites this size..."

"Could only have come from very big pests indeed," murmured Max. "Well, you're not the only one, Mr. Tompkins. Quite a lot of funny things have been happening recently."

Timmy was still holding the local newspaper, and Max showed Mr. Tompkins the strange stories.

As his father studied the paper, Timmy turned to Max. "All right then, what do you think is going on? I know you don't like the weather, but you can't blame all

12

this on the sunshine."

"Precisely!" said Max. "There's something else, some missing link…"

Mr. Tompkins looked up from the newspaper. "That's odd. That's very odd."

"That's what we're saying, Dad," said Timmy impatiently.

Mr. Tompkins shook his head. "No, you don't understand. What's really odd is that I know all these people. Sid Simmons who was stung. Charley Corbett whose boy was bitten, and Andy Brown the grocer. I know them all."

"Aha!" said Max. "And how do you know them?"

Mr. Tompkins looked puzzled. "I just know them, that's all."

"Think, Mr. Tompkins!" urged Max. "There must be some link."

"Well, Sid's in my garden club…of course! So are Charley Corbett and Andy

Brown! I know them all from the club!"

"Aha!" said Max. "Mr. Tompkins, would you have a list of your garden club members?"

"There's a club directory somewhere. I think I left it in the shed."

"I'd be awfully grateful if you could manage to find it for me."

"All right, I'll try to find it."

Looking thoroughly baffled, Mr. Tompkins went into the shed and started searching around.

Timmy turned to Max. "If the heat wave is causing these giant insects, what's causing the heat wave? And why should people in Dad's garden club have more trouble than anyone else?"

"Why, indeed?" said Max. "I think the strange weather and all these strange events are somehow connected."

"How?"

"My dear Timmy, that's what we've got to find out."

Mr. Tompkins came out of the shed.

He was walking very slowly backwards, there was a little booklet in his hand, and his face was a ghastly green color.

"What's the matter, Dad?" asked Timmy.

Mr. Tompkins tried to speak but he could only croak.

He pointed.

Stalking out of the shed after him was a giant spider!

Chapter Three

Timmy to the Rescue

The spider was huge—about the size of a cat or a small dog.

It had pincers in front, four pairs of legs, and its fat, round body, divided into two segments, had black and white markings. It marched slowly toward the terrified Mr. Tompkins.

Then, with amazing suddenness, it sprang!

Timmy reacted almost without thinking.

Mr. Tompkins's garden spade was leaning against the fence and Timmy grabbed it, whirled it around and walloped the spider while it was still in midair, like a baseball player hitting a home run.

The spider whizzed clear across the garden, slammed against the fence on the

other side and dropped to the ground.

Timmy ran across the garden, spade raised high like an axe. Then, slowly, he lowered it again. "It's all right. It seems to be dead."

"Well played, old chap," said Max.

"Thanks a lot, son," said Mr. Tompkins. "Glad I taught you how to play baseball!"

Timmy looked down at the dead spider. "Where did it come from?"

"It was under my workbench," said Mr. Tompkins. He laughed nervously. "Glad I didn't get stuck in its web!"

Max peered down at the spider. "I think you'll find that's a zebra spider. They don't make webs; they just jump on their prey."

"Do they really?" asked Mr. Tompkins faintly. "Here's that membership list you asked for." He handed Max the little booklet.

Max took it and studied it. "You wouldn't know which of your fellow members lives nearest?"

Mr. Tompkins considered. "That'd be Bob Benson on the next street. Quite a few of them live close by."

"Well, we must try to see as many as we can," said Max.

"I've got a town map in my room," said Timmy. "We can go on my bike."

They shoveled the spider into an empty paper bag, and put it back in Mr. Tompkin's shed.

"Do you think I should tell anyone about this?" asked Mr. Tompkins nervously.

"No, no," said Max. "Leave it to me for the moment."

"I'd give the gardening a rest for today, Dad," said Timmy.

Mr. Tompkins shuddered. "Don't worry. I'm thinking of giving it up altogether. I think I'll take your mother and Sam for a nice drive to the beach."

Before long Timmy and Max were gliding down the hot, sunny street, Timmy pedaling away and Max sitting behind him. They found Bob Benson, a plump jolly-looking man, in his front

yard sprinkling plant food from a paper sack all around the base of a giant rosebush.

He looked up when they arrived. "Morning, Mr. Benson," said Timmy, as he and Max got off the bike.

"Roses are doing well!"

"Never better, Timmy," said Mr. Benson cheerfully. "Whole garden's blooming, in spite of the heat. What can I do for you?"

At this point Max took over. "One or

two rather odd things have been happening to club members recently," he said smoothly. "We wondered if you'd had any strange experiences yourself."

Mr. Benson's friendly manner vanished at once. "Me? Certainly not! Now if you'll excuse me, I'm very busy."

Max stared hard at him, green eyes glowing hypnotically. "Are you quite sure, my dear fellow?" he purred. "I'm sure you'd feel better if you told us."

Mr. Benson stared into Max's eyes for a moment. Then he leaned forward, whispering confidentially. "It was last night, when I was coming home from the club. I admit I was sleepy, but I saw it, I tell you, clear as anything in the moonlight."

"Saw what?" asked Timmy.

"A giant slug on the garden path! It was enormous—big as a cushion! I ran in the house and locked myself in. Didn't dare tell anyone. They'd have thought I was crazy!"

They calmed Mr. Benson down and rode on their way.

They drew a blank with the next member, Mr. Caldicott, a thin bearded man. "Nothing strange in my garden, my boy. I'm an organic gardener. Natural manure, that's the thing! Hard to find these days."

Max cocked his head. "Is there a riding school near here? I could have sworn I heard the sound of horses' hooves."

"Horses," said Mr. Caldicott. "A

splendid source of natural organic manure."

Grabbing a shovel and a bucket, Mr. Caldicott rushed off.

They went to see two more garden club members, Mr. Potter and Mr. Meek.

After some gentle persuasion from Max, both admitted to strange experiences. Mr. Potter had been chased by a giant snail, and Mr. Meek had found a foot-long caterpillar munching on one of his cabbages. Neither man had told anyone for fear of not being believed.

It was tiring work riding around in the blazing sun. They bought a couple of cans of cold soda and went to consider their next move under a shady tree in the local part.

A wasp buzzed briefly around their soda cans, brightly colored butterflies were in the bushes, and ants marched around busily in the dust.

"At least all the insects seem to be normal size," said Timmy, looking around a little nervously.

Max sat hunched up under the tree, his chin in his paws. "That's what's so baffling, old chap. Why should this plague affect the members of one little garden club?"

"Not all of them. Nothing happened to Mr. Caldicott. Maybe giant insects don't like natural manure!"

"That's it!" said Max. "Who's in charge of this garden club?"

Timmy studied the booklet. "President Mr. Charles Chitterham, Chitterham Lodge." He looked at his map. "It's just on the other side of the park."

Max sprang to his feet. "Excellent! We must see him at once!"

"All right, Max, what's the sudden rush?"

Max was positively bouncing up and

down with excitement. "Don't you see, we've found the answer! All we need now is the proof."

Max jumped on the bike. "My turn to pedal, I think?"

Timmy jumped on behind, Max pedaled furiously, and they sped along the bicycle path like the wind.

Chapter Four

The Sinister Secret

When they reached Chitterham Lodge, a
large imposing white building, Max
parked the bike beside the front gate and
led the way around to the big greenhouse
in the back.

There were plants and flowers of all
kinds, and a sprinkler system filled the
warm air with a gentle spray.

Max paused by a bench with a row
of tomato plants, all bearing tiny
red tomatoes.

Beneath the bench was a row of strangely familiar-looking paper sacks.

"There you are," said Max. "The missing link we've been looking for!"

He opened one of the sacks—it was filled with grains of gray powder.

"There was a sack just like this in your father's shed. Mr. Benson was putting this stuff on his roses—and I bet Potter and Meek are using it too."

"But *not* Mr. Caldicott, who never uses chemicals at all."

Timmy looked at the sack. The words WIZZIGROW SAMPLE BATCH 8937Q were stenciled in black letters on the side. "Doesn't look like anything you'd buy in a garden center."

"Quite so. My theory is it's something new and experimental—and highly dangerous."

A puzzled voice behind them said, "What on earth are you fellows doing here?"

They turned and saw a tall sharp-nosed man staring down at them in amazement.

Immediately Max did one of his amazing personality changes.

Drawing himself up stiffly, he spoke in the droning voice of a petty official. "Mr. Charles Chitterham, I presume?"

"That's me, all right. But who are you?"

"I am from the Department of

Agriculture, sir. I am investigating the unauthorized use of a fertilizer known as Wizzigrow."

Mr. Chitterham looked shocked. "Unauthorized? I had no idea!"

Max licked the end of an imaginary pencil and prepared to take notes in an invisible notebook.

"Then may I inquire as to how the said fertilizing agent entered your possession?"

Mr. Chitterham seemed only too eager to explain. "I'm the president of the local garden club, you know."

"I am aware of that fact," said Max, in a voice that suggested he was aware of a great deal else as well. "Please continue!"

Now thoroughly daunted, Mr. Chitterham stammered, "Well, the makers of the stuff came to see me. Said they wanted to do a limited trial in the field—or rather in the garden!"

He gave a nervous laugh which died away under Max's cold green stare. He stumbled on. "Well, they offered quite a handsome cash donation to the club if our members would try it out. I put it to the members and most agreed— apart from one or two, who were a bit dubious."

"Such as Mr. Caldicott?"

"Yes, but how did you know?"

"Investigations *have* been in progress for some time," droned Max.

"I must inform you, sir, that you have committed an offense under Regulation 47B."

"I'm most terribly sorry. I had no idea!"

"Ignorance of the law is no excuse," said Max severely. "I must ask you to cease the use of this illegal substance and to request your members to do the same."

"Yes, of course, I'll do that immediately.

Should I contact the Wizzigrow people as well?"

"On no account," said Max severely. "I shall be dealing with them myself! Er…which address have you been dealing with?"

"The new factory in Totters Lane, just on the edge of town. But surely you knew that already?"

"Of course we knew!" said Max. "Just checking."

It was just before dark, and Timmy was crouching beside his bike in a ditch outside the Wizzigrow factory. It was a low, ultra-modern building, half-hidden in the woods, crowned with an enormous silver chimney and surrounded by a tall wire fence. Max, who'd been off scouting around, appeared silently beside him.

"Place is guarded like Fort Knox, dear

boy. Electrified fence, heat sensing devices. Going to be quite a job getting inside."

"Do we have to?" asked Timmy nervously.

"Oh, I think we'd better take a look, don't you? They can't be up to any good or they wouldn't be so secretive."

"I don't call that chimney secretive. You

can see it for miles."

"It's odd that chimney... Why is it so high?"

"Search me. There doesn't seem to be anything coming out of it."

Max stared up. "I'm not sure. There's a sort of shimmering at the top. I think something *is* coming out—something invisible—and deadly dangerous."

They heard a low rumbling, distant at first, but getting nearer.

"Quick," said Max. "This may be our chance!" He led Timmy toward the trees that clustered around the big main gate.

A huge delivery truck drew up outside the gate, and waited while the guard checked the driver's papers and phoned for instructions.

By now Max and Timmy were perched in the branches of a tree that overhung the gate.

As the truck revved up its engine they

dropped, first Max then Timmy, landing on the broad flat roof.

The gates swung open, the truck drove slowly through, and the gates closed again behind it.

"Well, we're in," thought Timmy. "I only hope we can get out again!"

Chapter Five

Max's Countdown

The truck followed a service road around to the back of the building and pulled up outside a loading bay. Men in protective suits appeared and began unloading sealed containers.

On the other side of them, Max sprang silently from the top of the truck. Timmy jumped and Max caught him, lowering him gently to the ground. They moved quitely away.

They turned the corner of the building

and found a locked metal door set low in the wall. Max stared hard at it, purring softly, his eyes glowing green. Something clicked inside the lock mechanism, the

door swung open and they slipped inside. They found themselves in a brightly lit factory area, moving between banks of mysteriously silent machinery. Thick, multicolored plastic pipes ran along the walls. Every now and then something would whirr, or click or gurgle.

"Where is everyone?" whispered Timmy.

"Automation, old chap," said Max. "Come on, let's try this way."

There was a heavy metal door in the far wall, held closed by a steel bar. Max lifted the bar and they went inside.

On the other side of the door was a long room which seemed to be a combination of laboratory, greenhouse and control room. There was a complicated-looking instrument console just inside the door. One side of the room was lined with glass-fronted cages, the

other with all kinds of plants, fruits and
vegetables, growing in huge metal trays.

Timmy peered in one of the cages and
gasped. "Max, look!"

From inside the cage, a huge ant was
waving its feelers at him. They looked in
the other cages. There were insects of
every kind—slugs, spiders, caterpillars,
wasps, worms, and snails—all grown to
enormous size.

Max moved over to the other side of
the room and studied one of the trays. It

contained a tomato plant, loaded down with huge, red, juicy tomatoes. Max took a pinch of soil from one of the trays. It was gray and lifeless.

"You see, Timmy? This is what happens if you keep on using that Wizzigrow stuff. It drains all the goodness from the soil—so the only way to grow *anything* will be to buy more and more Wizzigrow. And the more you use, the more you need!"

"Exactly," said a strangely familiar voice. "A bit tough on the farmers and gardeners—but *very* good for my company profits!"

A tall figure had entered the laboratory. It was Mr. Charles Chitterham, President of the garden club. Guards appeared in the doorway behind him, looking like aliens in their protective suits.

Mr. Chitterham smiled at the look of amazement on Timmy's face.

"You seem surprised to see me, young man. Did I forget to mention that I'm also President of Wizzigrow Incorporated?"

"I should have realized," said Max. "The tomatoes on your plant were normal size, and the sacks weren't even open. You weren't using the stuff, just distributing it."

"Oh, I don't use it myself," said Mr. Chitterham. "Unfortunate side effects in the garden pests department. Gets into the insect food chain, you see, and produces the odd mutation." He nodded toward the row of giant insects. "We're working on a special insecticide to control them—then we can sell that too!"

"There's another big problem too, isn't there?" asked Max.

Mr. Chitterham smiled. "You mean all the freon produced in making the stuff? Oh, it's harmless. You don't want to believe all this ecological rubbish!"

Timmy's class had just done a project on global warming.

"Freon? That's the stuff that weakens the ozone layer isn't it? And hangs around retaining heat. Is that why it's been so hot?"

"Exactly," said Max. "This factory has been pouring out so much freon through that chimney that your town's had its own private greenhouse effect!"

He looked sternly at Mr. Chitterham.

"You do realize that the manufacturing of Wizzigrow must cease immediately?"

"The only thing that's going to cease immediately is you, my interfering friends!" Mr. Chitterham pointed to the insect cages.

"The cages can be opened automatically from outside the laboratory. So I'm going to lock you in here and release the insects." He smiled evilly. "They're very hungry and they've all got big appetites. Some will eat the plants, and some will eat each other—but I'm afraid that some of them will eat you! It will be an interesting experiment."

Timmy shuddered.

Ignoring the gruesome threat, Max strolled up to the main control bank.

"Tricky business, making this Wizzigrow stuff, I imagine. Lots of dangerous chemicals, difficult process? Constant danger of explosions!"

"Nonsense!" snapped Mr. Chitterham. "It's perfectly safe!"

"Are you quite sure?" drawled Max. He folded his eyes and began to give a deep throbbing purr. He stared hard at the control bank, his eyes glowing green.

The control bank started to throb and hum. Lights flashed, dials flickered and the control room started to shudder.

"Doesn't look too safe to me," said Max, and went on purring.

Suddenly a cheerful computer voice filled the room. It was the kind of voice that tells you your plane has been canceled.

"Attention everyone. This installation has gone into overdrive and is about to explode. You are advised to leave immediately. Three minutes to explosion time and counting."

The guards looked uneasily at each other.

Mr. Chitterham leaped to the control console and began frantically pushing buttons and throwing switches.

The warning lights flashed even more wildly, and the throbbing grew louder.

"Two minutes to explosion time," said the computer voice happily. The guards turned and fled. Mr. Chitterham tried to

follow them, but the door had locked itself behind them.

"One minute to explosion," trilled the computer voice.

Max went on purring, staring hard at the console. "Won't be long now, old fellow—unless, of course, you'd like to promise to close down Wizzigrow."

"You're bluffing," screamed Mr. Chitterham.

("I hope so!" thought Timmy.)

"Bluffing? Not at all, my dear fellow," said Max. "Either you close it down or I blow it up!"

The throbbing in the control room grew louder and louder and the whole place shook.

"Forty-nine seconds, forty-eight seconds...," said the computer cheerfully. "The laboratory will explode in forty seconds precisely!"

When the countdown reached thirty

seconds Mr. Chitterham gave up. "All right, all right! I'll do anything you say!"

"Fifteen seconds to explosion time!"

Max stopped purring. He yawned and blinked.

Slowly the throbbing from the control bank died away.

"Countdown arrested at nine seconds," said the computer voice happily. "Have a nice day!"

Timmy's dad looked up from the latest edition of the local newspaper.

"Mr. Chitterham has resigned as President of our garden club. Apparently he's retiring from the business early. Going to live abroad, due to nervous strain."

"Really?" drawled Max.

"All that Wizzigrow stuff was collected and destroyed, you know." Mr. Tompkins went on. "They've closed down the whole factory."

"Any giant insect stories?" asked Timmy.

"Not a single one."

"I imagine they've all died out, now that their Wizzigrow's cut off," said Max.

A rumble of thunder shook the kitchen

window, and big drops spattered against the pane.

"Looks as if the fine weather's broken," said Mr. Tompkins.

"Never mind, Dad," said Timmy. "A drop of rain will be good for the garden!"

About the Author

After studying at Cambridge, Terrance Dicks became an advertising copywriter, then a radio and television scriptwriter and script editor. His career as an author began with the *Dr. Who* series and he has now written a variety of other books on subjects ranging from horror to detection. Barron's publishes several of his series, including *The Adventures of Goliath*, *T.R. Bear*, *A Cat Called Max*, and *The MacMagics*.

More Exciting Adventures With Arch Books

Arch Books are Barron's gripping mini-novels for children of various reading ages. Each of the titles in this series offers the young reader a special adventure. The stories are packed with action, humor, mystery, chilling thrills and even a bit of magic! Each paperback book boasts 12 to 24 handsome line-art illustrations. Each book: $2.95, Can. $3.95 (those marked with an * are $3.50, Can. $4.25.) (Ages 6–11)

Arch Book Titles:

BEN AND THE CHILD OF THE FOREST
ISBN: 3936-X

THE BLUEBEARDS: Adventure on Skull Island
ISBN: 4421-5

THE BLUEBEARDS: Mystery at Musket Bay
ISBN: 4422-3

THE BLUEBEARDS: Peril at the Pirate School
ISBN: 4502-5

THE BLUEBEARDS: Revenge at Ryan's Reef*
ISBN: 4903-9

CAROLINE MOVES IN
ISBN: 3938-6

A CAT CALLED MAX: Magnificent Max
ISBN: 4427-4

A CAT CALLED MAX: Max and the Quiz Kids
ISBN: 4501-7

A CAT CALLED MAX: Max's Amazing Summer*
ISBN: 4819-9

IN CONTROL, MS. WIZ?
ISBN: 4500-9

INTO THE NIGHT HOUSE
ISBN: 4423-1

MEET THE MACMAGICS*
ISBN: 4882-2

MS. WIZ SPELLS TROUBLE
ISBN: 4420-7

THE MACMAGICS: A Spell for My Sister*
ISBN: 4881-4

THE MACMAGICS: My Brother the Vampire*
ISBN: 4883-0

THE RED SPORTS CAR
ISBN: 3937-8

YOU'RE UNDER ARREST, MS. WIZ
ISBN: 4499-1

All prices are in U.S. and Canadian dollars and subject to change without notice. At your bookstore or order direct adding 10% postage (minimum charge $1.75 — Canada $2.00). N.Y. residents add sales tax. ISBN PREFIX: 0-8120

Barron's Educational Series, Inc.
250 Wireless Blvd., Hauppauge, NY 11788
Call toll-free: 1-800-645-3476
In Canada: Georgetown Book Warehouse,
34 Armstrong Ave., Georgetown, Ont. L7G 4R9
Call toll-free: 1-800-247-7160

More Fun, Mystery, And Adventure With Goliath–

Goliath's Birthday*
Goliath's fifth birthday is here. My, how dog years fly! A party is planned but will it go off without a hitch or will Goliath be his mischievous self? (Paperback only, ISBN: 4821-0)

Teacher's Pet*
David helps save his teacher Mr. Paine with the kind of help that only Goliath can give! (Paperback only, ISBN: 4820-2)

Goliath And The Burglar
The first Goliath story tells how Goliath becomes a hero when he saves his new family from a nasty burglar! (Paperback, ISBN 3820-7—Library Binding, ISBN 5823-2)

Goliath And The Buried Treasure
When Goliath discovers how much fun it is to dig holes, both he and David get into trouble with the neighbors, until Goliath's skill at digging transforms him into the most unlikely hero in town! (Paperback, ISBN 3819-3—Library Binding, ISBN 5822-4)

Goliath On Vacation
David persuades his parents to bring Goliath with them on vacation—but the big hound quickly disrupts life at the hotel. (Paperback, ISBN 3821-5—Library Binding, ISBN 5824-0)

Goliath At The Dog Show
Goliath helps David solve the mystery at the dog show—then gets a special prize for his effort! (Paperback, ISBN 3818-5—Library Binding, ISBN 5821-6)

Goliath's Christmas
Goliath plays a big part in rescuing a snowstorm victim. Then he and David join friends for the best Christmas party ever. (Paperback, ISBN 3878-9—Library Binding, ISBN 5843-7)

Goliath's Easter Parade
With important help from Goliath, David finds a way to save the neighborhood playground by raising funds at the Easter Parade. (Paperback, ISBN 3957-2—Library Binding, ISBN 5877-1)

Goliath And The Cub Scouts
Mystery abounds when David and his big, loveable dog Goliath attend a Cub Scouts meeting in a gym where a mysterious burglary takes place. Can Goliath help David solve the mystery? (Paperback only, ISBN 4493-2)

Written by Terrance Dicks and illustrated by Valerie Littlewood. Goliath books are in bookstores, or order direct from Barron's. Paperbacks $2.95 each, Library Bindings $7.95 each. (If marked with an * then price is $3.50. No Canadian Rights.) When ordering direct from Barron's, please indicate ISBN number and add 10% postage and handling (Minimum $1.75, Can. $2.00). N.Y. residents add sales tax. ISBN PREFIX: 0-8120

250 Wireless Boulevard, Hauppauge, NY 11788
Call toll free: 1-800-645-3476